DURHAM PUBLIC LI

CatDog's Big Idea

If you purchased this book without a cover you should be
aware that this book is stolen property. It was reported as
"unsold and destroyed" to the publisher and neither the author
nor the publisher has received any payment for
this "stripped book."

Based on the TV series *CatDog*®
created by Peter Hannan as seen on Nickelodeon®

Editorial Consultants: Peter Hannan and Robert Lamoreaux
Additional assistance provided by the CatDog Production Team.

SIMON SPOTLIGHT
An imprint of Simon & Schuster Children's Publishing Division
1230 Avenue of the Americas, New York, New York 10020

Copyright © 1999 Viacom International Inc.
All rights reserved. NICKELODEON, *CatDog*, and all related titles, logos,
and characters are trademarks of Viacom International Inc.

All rights reserved including the right of reproduction in whole or in part in any form.

SIMON SPOTLIGHT and colophon are registered trademarks of Simon & Schuster.

Produced by Bumpy Slide Books
Designed by sheena needham • ess design and development
Manufactured in the United States of America

First Edition
2 4 6 8 10 9 7 5 3 1

Library of Congress Cataloging-in-Publication Data
Braybrooks, Ann.
CatDog's big idea / by Ann Braybrooks and Eliot Brown;
illustrated by Niall Harding. —1st Simon Spotlight ed.
p. cm. —(Ready-to-read. Level 2, Reading together)
Summary: CatDog, an animal who is half cat, half dog, devises a bold
scheme to get back a bicycle stolen by the Greasers, but the plan goes awry.
ISBN 0-689-83005-X (pbk.)
[1. Cats—Fiction. 2. Dogs—Fiction. 3.Bicycles and
bicycling—Fiction.] I. Braybrooks, Ann. II. Harding, Niall, ill.
III. CatDog (Television program). IV. Title. V. Series
PZ7.B73884Cat 1999
[Fic] 21 99-24001
CIP

by Ann Braybrooks and Eliot Brown
illustrated by Niall Harding

JEZ
BRAYBROOKS

Ready-to-Read

Simon Spotlight/Nickelodeon

One morning, CatDog jumped on their bike. They headed to town.

"Hi-ho-diggety!" shouted Dog. "Isn't this fun?"

Suddenly, Cliff, Lube, and Shriek ran out from behind some bushes and blocked the road.

"Greaser alert!" Cat yelled. "Hit the brakes, Dog!"

But Dog couldn't stop in time. The Greasers tied CatDog into a knot. Then they grabbed the bike.

"Looks like we got us a new Greasermobile!" Cliff declared. Then the Greasers rode away and left CatDog in the dust.

CatDog walked home. In their living room, Winslow asked, "What's eating you two?"

"The Greasers stole our bike," Cat said. "And there's nothing we can do. They are so much stronger than us."

"Sheesh," said Winslow, "too bad you're not smart enough to think of a way to get your bike back! Heh, Heh!"

"That's it!" Cat cried. "Maybe if I were *smarter*, I could figure out a way to make Dog *stronger*. Then we could get our bike back."

"Yeah, right," laughed Winslow.

Cat picked up the phone and dialed.
"Hello?" he said. "Einstein's Outlet? I'd
like to order a set of Happy Brain videos."

When the videos arrived, Cat watched them all. Then he watched them again. Soon his brain began to grow.

"Good news," Cat said the next day. "I've come up with a plan. I have created a potion that will give Dog the strength of 10,000 Greasers."

"I'm thirsty," Dog said. "Can I drink it now?"

"Sure," Cat replied. "Here you go. The effects will only last exactly thirty-seven minutes and four seconds. And you must NOT eat any fruit."

"Why?" asked Dog.

"Because fruit makes you big and strong," said Cat. "And if we mix my potion with fruit, you could become *too* big and strong!"

"Now here's the rest of my plan," Cat said. "Winslow, I need you to keep the Greasers busy. Then Dog and I will take back our bicycle."

"What's in this for me?" asked Winslow.

"A brand-new car!" Cat cried. "Say 'hello' to your new Robo-CatDog 3000! I made it myself. It's easy when you have the brains."

"Cool!" cried Winslow. "I have always wanted my own set of wheels!"

Winslow jumped into the driver's seat. Cat started the car. The "RCD 3000" roared to life with a *v-room*!

Cat turned to Dog. "How do you
feel?" he asked.

"Bigger," answered Dog.

"Good!" Cat said. "All right,
everybody, let's hit the road. . . ."

But it was too late. Winslow was
already gone in a cloud of fumes.

"Can I please chase a garbage truck?"
Dog begged.

"No! We have to stick to the plan. I'm
getting crushed down here," Cat said.

"It was your idea to make me bigger,"
Dog told him.

"And it was a smart idea!" Cat replied.

Back at the Greasers' house, Cliff, Lube, and Shriek had just come home.

"Is there anything to eat?" asked Lube.

"No," replied Shriek. "You ate the last of the pizza for breakfast!"

"Oh, yeah. I forgot," Lube said. Then he started to look in the sofa for leftovers.

Suddenly, Lube saw the RCD 3000 pull into the yard. "Hey guys," he called, "CatDog just showed up on our front lawn!"

"I love it when *they* come to *us*," said Cliff. "Let's get 'em!"

The Greasers chased the RCD 3000 down the street. Then CatDog tried to slip into the house. . . .

"Cat, I'm stuck," Dog said.

"Wait here!" Cat said.

Cat disappeared into the Greaser's garage. In no time, he invented something to cut a bigger doorway for Dog to fit through.

"There's our bike!" said Cat. "Let's grab it! We don't have much time left. You're going to shrink back to normal soon."

"Shrink?" asked Dog. "Cat, I seem to be *growing*."

Cat was surprised. "That doesn't make sense. Did you eat anything?"

"Well, I did just lick a pillow. It tasted like pizza," Dog said. "It was spicy!"

"Pizza?" cried Cat. "It has tomato sauce!"

"Whew!" said Dog. "Thank goodness tomatoes are only vegetables."

"Tomatoes are fruit!" exclaimed Cat. "Fruit makes you bigger and stronger!"

"Aaarrgghh!" they screamed together.

Suddenly, Cat started to feel dizzy.

"Oh, no!" Cat cried. "The warning on the videos said if I didn't keep watching them, I would lose my smarts! Grab the bike. Quick!"

Just then, Winslow drove by the house in the RCD 3000. The Greasers were right behind him.

"Hey, look!" shouted Shriek. "Cat's got *our* bike! We've been tricked!"

The Greasers jumped on Cat. They
tried to take the bike away from him.

"Hey, wait a minute!" Shriek cried.
"Something's wrong here. Where's his
other half?"

Suddenly Dog burst out of the house!
"Aahhh!" yelled the Greasers. They ran
for their lives!

Screech! Winslow lost control of the RCD 3000 and ran right over Cat's foot.

"Ow! Ow! Ow!" cried Cat.

"Yikes!" cried Winslow as Dog came toppling down on the Robo-CatDog 3000 and CatDog's bike.

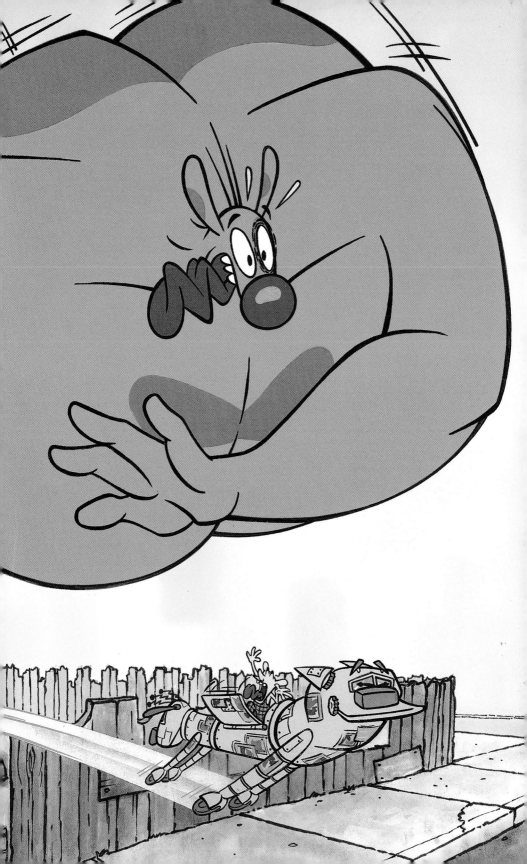

That night, Dog's body was its normal size again. Cat had his normal cat brain. And the doctor said Winslow would be better in no time.

"The Greasers are gonna kill you for wrecking their house," said Winslow.

"Yeah," said Cat. "But at least we got our bike back!"